SARATOGA   MAY 16 '74

J E
La Farge
Joanna

353587

495

J E   LA FARGE
           JOANNA RUNS
AWAY

353587 ✓

JOANNA
RUNS AWAY

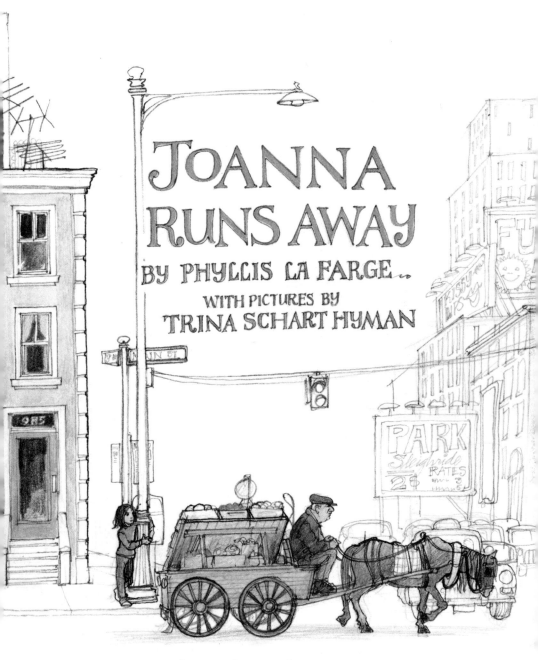

JOANNA RUNS AWAY

BY PHYLLIS LA FARGE

WITH PICTURES BY TRINA SCHART HYMAN

Holt, Rinehart and Winston

New York   Chicago   San Francisco

For Hilary...P.L.F.

For Gaby...T.S.H.

A Holt Reinforced Edition

Text copyright ©1973 by Phyllis La Farge Johnson
Illustrations copyright ©1973 by Trina Schart Hyman

Published simultaneously in Canada by
Holt, Rinehart and Winston of Canada, Limited.

ISBN: 0-03-091306-3
Library of Congress Catalog Card Number: 72-76579

Printed in the United States of America
First Edition
Designed by Aileen Friedman

Library of Congress Cataloging in Publication Data

La Farge, Phyllis.
    Joanna runs away.
    SUMMARY: Almost without meaning to, a little girl
tries to make her special daydream about the vegetable
man's cart horse come true.
    [1. City and town life—Fiction. 2. Horses—
Stories] I. Hyman, Trina Schart, illus. II. Title.
PZ7.L139Jo   [E]   72-76579
ISBN 0-03-091306-3

CONTENTS

CONSTANZA

Joanna loved animals.

She loved Roger, her gerbil.

She loved Cleo, Rex, and Ruby,

her guinea pigs.

She loved the animals in the zoo.

But it was a long ride on the subway

to get to the zoo.

On the weekend, Joanna's mother

never seemed to have time to take her.

During the week, Joanna went to school,

and her mother went to work.

Joanna loved the dogs in her building.

She loved Miss Shawn's poodle

and Mr. Emberley's dachshund.

But more than any other animal

Joanna loved Costanza.

Costanza was a horse.

She belonged to Mr. Lauro.

She pulled his vegetable wagon.

Every Wednesday,

once spring came,

Costanza came clip-clopping

down Joanna's street.

Joanno started waiting

for Costanza

the minute she was home from school.

When she heard the horse's clip-clop,

she took two lumps of sugar,

the list her mother had made that morning

and the money her mother had left for her.

Joanna said hi to Mr. Lauro,

but she did not read him

her mother's list right away.

She waited until all the other people

4

had bought what they wanted.

That way she had plenty of time

to pat Costanza

and to feed her the lumps of sugar.

Joanna liked Mr. Lauro.

He was old.

Her mother had told her that

he was the last of his kind.

Joanna wasn't sure

what this meant.

Maybe when he stopped

coming around,

no one would take his place.

She hoped that he wouldn't stop

while she was still a child,

because if he did,

she would have no chance

to see a horse.

Costanza was the only horse

she had ever seen.

Sometimes Joanna asked Mr. Lauro

if Costanza needed a drink of water.

Then he would fetch a water bucket

from the back of the wagon.

"Good girl," he would say.

"You make me remember my horse."

But he always laughed just a little
and made Joanna feel shy.
When it was time for him to go,
Mr. Lauro didn't even say good-bye,
but Joanna always called,
"See you next week."

After Mr. Lauro had gone, Joanna felt sad.

On other afternoons she played with Roger

or with Cleo and Rex and Ruby.

Or she went upstairs one flight

to see Miss Shawn,

or up two flights to see Mr. Emberley.

Sometimes she went downstairs

to see the Martin family,

but not for very long.

There were four children

in the Martin family.

They were used to being all together.

They did not mind a lot of noise.

On Wednesdays, after Mr. Lauro had gone,

Joanna just stayed by herself.

She thought about what it was like

to be all by yourself.

It seemed to her that things would be better

if she could live with Costanza.

But when she thought

about living with Costanza,

Costanza was not pulling

a vegetable wagon anymore.

Costanza and Joanna were in a green field,

and the sun was shining.

Jimmy

One Wednesday, after Mr. Lauro had gone,

Joanna was sitting dreaming about Costanza

when there was a knock at the door.

It was Jimmy Martin.

Joanna knew Jimmy felt all by himself

just the way she did.

His big brother played out in the street,

and his twin sisters were babies.

Joanna knew Jimmy wanted her

to play with him,

but he was younger than she was,

and he was a boy.

"Now I have an animal, too," Jimmy said.

The Martins had no animals.

"I have a turtle.

And I have turtle food to feed it."

He was carrying the turtle

in a plastic turtle dish.

14

"He's nice," Joanna said,

"but turtles don't live long on turtle food."

"But this is good turtle food," said Jimmy.

"My mother bought it for me at the store."

"I'm just telling you

what my teacher told me," said Joanna.

"Turtles don't live long on turtle food."

"They do so," said Jimmy.

"This turtle is going to live forever."

Then he ran out the door.

When he had gone,

Joanna tried to think about Costanza again.

But she couldn't.

For the next few days,

Joanna kept thinking about Jimmy,

but she did not go to see him,

and he did not come to see her.

Runaway Joanna

Then Wednesday came again.

It was a hot day.

School was almost over.

More then ever, Joanna wanted

Costanza and Mr. Lauro to come.

It would be the first nice thing

that had happened in a week.

While she was waiting,

Jimmy knocked at her door.

"What's good for turtles

if it's not turtle food?" he asked.

"My turtle is sick. Feel his shell."

Joanna touched the turtle's shell.

It was very soft.

Just then she heard Costanza's clip-clop.

"I don't know," Joanna said.

"I mean I can't tell you now.

Costanza is coming."

Joanna grabbed her mother's list

and the money

and the sugar cubes, and ran downstairs.

Jimmy looked after her

from the door of the apartment.

"I'll wait for you," he called.

Joanna patted Costanza

and fed her the sugar.

"I'm glad to see you, Costanza," she said.

"Are you glad to see me?"

Then Joanna did a strange thing.

She took a look

to see what Mr. Lauro was doing.

He was filling a bag

with artichokes for Miss Shawn.

Joanna slipped behind the wagon.

Looking quickly this way and that,

she climbed onto the wagon

and hid under the frame

that held the vegetables.

Mr. Lauro's scale rattled

just a few inches

from where she crouched.

She thought maybe she should climb out,

but she was afraid

that someone would see her

and ask her what she was doing.

I can always get out

when he stops again, she thought.

Then people won't know me,

and I can just go home.

Then she remembered the list and the money.

She felt for them in her pocket.

I'll give him the list

when I get out, she thought.

He won't remember what street I live on.

But when Mr. Lauro stopped,

there was never a moment when he

or one or two of his customers

were not standing at the end of the wagon.

And then the wagon

did not stop anymore.

Mr. Lauro just kept going.

Clip-clop, clip-clop,

went Costanza's hooves;

the wagon swayed and jounced

as it went over a bump

or a hole in the pavement.

The streets were hot and noisy.

Each time they stopped for a light,

Joanna peered out the back of the wagon

and thought about jumping down.

But she didn't.

Now they were traveling

through parts of Brooklyn

she did not know.

She was scared.

She saw an ice cream man in his truck,

but he was not the ice cream man

who came to her street.

She saw a church

that looked like a church she had seen once

when she was going someplace

with her mother,

but she was not sure it was the same one.

28

After a while, they had gone so far

that there were no more big buildings

but little houses

with small yards around them.

Pretty soon we will be in the country,

Joanna thought.

She felt a lot better.

That's why I'm here,

she said to herself.

I'm going to find Costanza a green field.

But they rode on and on,

and the country never came.

At last they turned.

Costanza pulled the wagon

a few yards more.

Then she stopped and Mr. Lauro jumped down.

Joanna peeped out

and saw him open the doors of a shed.

Costanza pulled the wagon into the shed.

Mr. Lauro unhitched her and led her away.

Then he began to lift

the boxes of vegetables and fruits

off the rack above Joanna.

30

Any moment he would see her.

She was thinking of giving herself up,

but just then she noticed a narrow angle

where the rack joined the wagon.

Quietly Joanna crawled in there

and lay still.

At last Mr. Lauro left the shed.

Joanna was alone.

She heard a door bang;

probably he had gone into his house.

All at once Joanna wanted to be home.

Was Mother worrying about her?

She felt the money

and the list in her pocket.

How much time had gone by

since she left the house?

Then she remembered Jimmy.

Was he still waiting for her?

Maybe his turtle was already dead.

Just then Costanza snorted quietly.

Joanna crawled down from the wagon.

She found Costanza in a stall

at the back of the shed.

She did not seem surprised to see Joanna.

Joanna put her arms around the horse's neck.

She forgot about Jimmy.

She told Costanza

that they were going to escape together

and look for the country.

"We're going to find

a green place for you, Costanza," she said.

Joanna sat down on a heap of straw.

It was hot in the shed,

although by now it was evening.

In spite of herself,

Joanna felt sleepy.

She stretched out comfortably

on the straw....

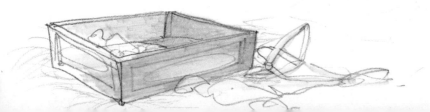

MR. LAURO

When Joanna awakened, it was dark outside.

She did not know where she was.

Then she smelled the straw

and smelled Costanza.

She jumped up.

She opened the gate to Costanza's stall.

"Come on, Costanza," she said.

"It's time to go."

Slowly Costanza followed Joanna

out of the stall

and past the wagon

and a big refrigerator.

They stopped at the door.

Joanna peeked out.

There was no one in the yard.

It was very quiet.

"Okay, Costanza," Joanna whispered.

"Let's go."

Clip-clop, clip-clop,

went Costanza's hooves.

"Don't make so much noise, Costanza,"

whispered Joanna.

"Ssh."

Clip-clop, clip-clop,

went Costanza.

They passed alongside

Mr. Lauro's house.

The television was gabbling loudly.

Maybe no one would hear them.

"Hurry, Costanza," she said.

"Let's get away from here."

But when they were a few feet

from the sidewalk,

Costanza stopped.

Joanna tried to push her,

but Costanza was far bigger

and stronger than she.

Costanza would not move another inch.

"Don't you want to be free?"

Joanna whispered fiercely.

"Do you want to stay

in that hot old stall forever?

Do you want to get old and die

pulling that wagon around stinky Brooklyn?"

Costanza stood for a moment longer.

Then she swung around

and headed back toward the shed.

Clip-clop, clip-clop, went her hooves.

At that moment

a long rectangle of light

shone suddenly

on the grass behind the house.

"Swear I heard that horse,"

Joanna heard Mr. Lauro's voice saying.

Next thing he had seen them both.

"What's going on?

Get back in your stall, old girl.

And who are you?"

Mr. Lauro grabbed Joanna

and pulled her along with him

while he drove Costanza back into the shed.

He switched on the light

and took a good look at Joanna.

"It's just a kid," he said.

"Someplace I've seen you.

Aren't you the girl

who always wants me

to give my horse a drink?"

Joanna nodded.

"But what are you doing here?

What are you doing with Costanza?

You didn't think

you could steal her, did you?"

"I wasn't trying to steal her,"

said Joanna,

"at least, not exactly.

I was trying to set her free.

I was going to find

a nice green field

for her and me to live in."

Mr. Lauro began to laugh,

a quiet laugh, not mean.

"A green field?" he asked.

"This is Brooklyn,

and there haven't been any fields here

since I've been here,

and I've been here forty years."

"I know," said Joanna.

"I wasn't really thinking.

It was a sort of dream."

"And besides," said Mr. Lauro,

"what would I do without Costanza?

I'm an old man.

I live by myself.

Costanza is all I've got."

"I didn't think of that," said Joanna.

"I didn't know you were all by yourself.

So am I.

I mean

my mother works all day."

"A little kid," Mr. Lauro said,

"all by herself."

He shook his head.

"We should be calling your mother.

She will be pretty worried."

They went into Mr. Lauro's house

and called Joanna's mother.

She sounded more worried than mad.

She said she would come right out,

but Mr. Lauro said

he would bring Joanna home.

47

He hitched Costanza to the wagon.

This time Joanna rode up front,

right next to Mr. Lauro.

She loved the lights and the darkness.

The ride home was the most wonderful thing

that had ever happened to her.

"Don't run away again, kid," Mr. Lauro said
when they were nearly home.

"I wasn't running away," said Joanna.

Then she added,

"Well, maybe I was."

"There's got to be someone

you could play with

till your mama gets home," said Mr. Lauro.

Joanna thought for a minute.

Then she said, "Maybe there is."

When they reached her street,

everyone was waiting for her:

Miss Shawn,

Mr. Emberley,

the Martin family,

and out in front, her mother.

Her mother hugged her, everyone hugged her.

For a while, Mr. Lauro stood around

telling his part of the story.

Then he said good-bye to Joanna.

"See you next week," he said.

"See you next week," Joanna replied.

Costanza clip-clopped into the darkness.

One by one, people said good night

and went indoors to their apartments.

Joanna and her mother went upstairs.

On the way up, Joanna put

her hand in her pocket.

Her mother's list and the money

were still there.

She took them out.

"I never bought what you wanted," she said.

Her mother gave her another hug.

Then Joanna thought of Jimmy.

She realized that

he had not been out on the street

when she arrived home.

"I've got to see Jimmy,"

she said to her mother.

"And I've got to buy him something."

"He was here when I came home,"

her mother said.

"He was worrying about something."

They went downstairs.

"Jimmy's mad at you,"

said Mrs. Martin.

"He says you stood him up."

Joanna walked past Mrs. Martin

into the back bedroom

where Jimmy slept

with his big brother.

"Is your turtle still alive?" she asked.

Jimmy nodded, but he didn't say anything.

55

"Fresh hamburger is what he needs,

and liver and lettuce.

Cut up in little bits.

That's what my teacher said.

I'll help you get some tomorrow."

"You really will?" asked Jimmy.

"I really will," said Joanna.

And then she went back upstairs

with her mother

and went to bed.

The End

ABOUT THE AUTHOR

Phyllis La Farge's articles have been featured in several national magazines. In 1965 she published her first book, *Kate and the Wild Kittens*. JOANNA RUNS AWAY is her fifth book for young readers. In addition, she is the author of an adult book of essays entitled *Keeping Going*.

For several years Phyllis La Farge and her family lived in Brooklyn, New York. Each week, a horse-drawn vegetable cart came through their street. Her memories of that horse and cart were the catalyst for this story. Today the author lives in Connecticut with her husband and their two children.

ABOUT THE ILLUSTRATOR

Trina Schart Hyman studied art at the Philadelphia Museum School, the Boston Museum School, and the Swedish State Art School. She began her career as an illustrator when she was eighteen years old. To date, her sprightly line drawings have brightened more than three dozen books for young readers.

Ms. Hyman lives in a 150-year-old house, on a "fantastically beautiful piece of northern New Hampshire wilderness," together with her daughter, an artist friend, two princesses, two dogs, a goat, a sheep, and eight cats.

ABOUT THE BOOK

The artwork is done in pencil and pen-and-ink, and was preseparated for two colors. The story was set in Caledonia linofilm type. The book was printed by offset.